Fantomina

or,

Love in a Maze

ELIZA HAYWOOD

WITH AN INTRODUCTION BY
Sarah R. Creel, Bethany E. Qualls
and Anna K. Sagal

RENARD PRESS

RENARD PRESS LTD

Kemp House
152–160 City Road
London EC1V 2NX
United Kingdom
info@renardpress.com
020 8050 2928

www.renardpress.com

Fantomina, or, Love in a Maze first published in 1725
This edition first published by Renard Press Ltd in 2021

Cover design by Will Dady

ISBN: 978-1-80447-006-0

CONTENTS

INTRODUCTION

*by Sarah R. Creel, Bethany E. Qualls
and Anna K. Sagal*

There is more to say about Eliza Haywood (née Fowler) than could possibly fit into an introduction, but suffice it to say that she is an eighteenth-century author whose body of work is incredibly expansive, yet only recently has scholarly attention been turned her way. In fact, Eliza Haywood is having a bit of a moment. *Fantomina*, in particular, has become a familiar text within the university classroom for its enduring tropes and fascinating titular character. This edition aims *Fantomina* (first published in 1725) at an even broader audience – bringing Haywood's imaginative and complex story squarely into the twenty-first century at a moment when she's sorely needed, both for her witty narrative capacity and for her shrewd exposé of women's lives and how they struggle(d) against a patriarchal system that held few, if any, opportunities for them.

So who was this woman whose oeuvre so delights and fascinates us today, but who only recently became part of a wider literary conversation? It is largely assumed that Eliza Haywood was born around 1693, but we do not know for certain. We do know that she died on the 25th of February 1756, aged somewhere around 60–63. She was buried in St Margaret's churchyard, Westminster, with no known grave marker, while many of her male predecessors, contemporaries and successors are enshrined in the illustrious Poet's Corner in Westminster Abbey.

Of unknown parentage, Haywood entered the historical record in 1714 in the cast lists of Smock Alley Theatre in Dublin. At this point, she was using the surname 'Haywood', but a husband of the same name has not been found in any historical register. Two letters from the late 1720s indicate that she had two children, but about as much is known of them as Mr Haywood. As this brief biography suggests, details about Haywood's personal life are frustratingly scant, and literary scholars and historians alike have combed the inner recesses of libraries and private collections, trying to find out more about her – anything to help us better understand one of the most prolific writers of the eighteenth century. But Haywood herself requested that her letters be destroyed at the end of her life – a move that makes it difficult to discover more personal facts about her.

While we may not be able to piece together many details of Haywood's life, her body of work speaks for itself. Shortly after her time in Dublin as an actress, Haywood began writing works of fiction in an 'amatory' style (described in more detail below), as was popular at the time. Writing for money how-ever, was not a respectable career for a woman in the eighteenth century, and, well, one might see how writing tales of seduction would not necessarily add credence to her reputation. But Eliza Haywood shirked the typical her entire life. She tended to follow trends rather than bow to societal pressure, a characteristic that scholars and fans of her work find both charming and frustrating, as later in her life she switched to writing in a more religious 'conduct book' style, often correcting and admonishing her earlier amatory characters in her later work.

Not much about Eliza Haywood's life, or even her work, is easy to understand. Yet her work chal-lenges, captivates and shows us that she was an author who expanded herself *alongside* the literary marketplace, leaving us with works like *Fantomina* that continue to delight and mystify.

While *Fantomina* is unarguably a compelling text for modern readers, some contextualisation of significant socio-cultural differences between the twenty-first and eighteenth centuries are useful for a contemporary audience.

The novella's depiction of human sexuality – male and female – draws upon several widely circulating stereotypes of masculinity and femininity. We begin by meeting the unnamed narrator, a wealthy ingénue who has been raised in the country but is now spending her time mostly unsupervised in London. For eighteenth-century readers, this would have immediately raised some red flags. She is understandably intrigued by the sophisticated, fashionable world of London, but as 'a Stranger to the World', she is unable to appropriately respond to the social dynamics of the theatre crowd and its sexual undercurrents. Deciding to dress 'in the Fashion of those Women who make sale of their Favours' (i.e. prostitutes) is framed as 'the Gratification of an Innocent Curiosity'. However, as any regular reader of fiction in the period would have known, this small misstep will inevitably lead to greater sins. Haywood differs from many of her fellow authors by assigning blame for this error in judgement not only to the pseudonymous female protagonist, but also to her conveniently absent London aunt, who is supposed to chaperone the young country lady, and to her recurrent seducer Beauplaisir.

Beauplaisir represents a popular model of risqué masculinity in eighteenth-century literature: the rake. The figure of the rake or libertine evoked for readers a charming, sexually assertive man whose desires were not shaped by marriage, respect for women or social propriety. Beauplaisir (whose Francophone name signals 'good pleasure' – a helpful clue that his most meaningful character trait is his interest in amorous affairs) isn't among the worst of the eighteenth-century libertines in fiction, but he does pursue multiple sexual relationships with the protagonist, believing her to embody various sexual archetypes: the courtesan, the housemaid, the widow and a glamorously elusive wealthy woman. The pursuit of extramarital or recreational sex does not automatically confer the status of libertine on a man;

in fact, male infidelity in aristocratic marriages was not uncommon, and, unlike their wives, husbands had relative legal and social laxity when it came to extracurricular activities. Where Beauplaisir is most at fault, according to Fantomina and to Haywood, is in the ease with which he discards sexual partners in favour of someone new and more sexually exciting (the irony being that none of these 'new' sexual partners actually is).

In adopting each of these characters to sexually attract Beauplaisir, Fantomina demonstrates a greater awareness of sexual modes of performance than her initial inability to recognise the women in the theatre box as prostitutes would suggest. Haywood, at least, knows that her readers would be able to interpret the character's rotating disguises as a series of recognisable models of appealing femininity. While prevailing social codes regarding female sexuality and feminine expression of desire absolutely condemned Fantomina's pursuit of physical pleasure, there is also a clear indication that Haywood wants us to admire Fantomina's cleverness and to recognise the very real frustration she feels as a (repeatedly) betrayed woman.

In fact, one of Haywood's recurring concerns in fiction is the vulnerable social position of women in eighteenth-century society and the dangers of their precarious economic and legal status. Many of her novels recount stories of female characters abused, betrayed, abandoned and victimised by a variety of horrible men. Unfortunately, there were very few legitimate ways for women to respond to male betrayal. A few, like the Baroness de Tortillée in *The Injur'd Husband* (1722), take vengeance into their own hands, but in doing so become infamous villains. Simultaneously, however, Haywood was aware of the role that women could play in their own safety; it is no coincidence that many of her less fortunate female characters who meet bad ends are occasionally complicit in their own demise. More broadly, Haywood's other writing, like *Epistles for the Ladies* (1749) and *The Female Spectator* (1744–46), use a shorter essay form to address various social, political and sexual politics, emphasising the importance of women looking after other women – ultimately, men cannot be trusted to do so.

Haywood's fiction and non-fiction writings provide an enlightening perspective on eighteenth-century sexuality that can surprise many modern readers.

While twenty-first-century readers may assume that people in the past (especially anything much earlier than the mid-twentieth century) were sexually repressed and/or limited by conservative social conventions, this generalisation elides the complicated history of human sexuality. It is true that various religious, legal and social conventions dictated the kinds of sexual expression that were publicised and broadly endorsed. However, the range of intimacies practiced by real people in the eighteenth century – as well as the kinds of writing and art that focused on sex – was much more diverse and progressive. Social gatherings like masquerades, in which male and female attendees dressed in costume to obscure their identities, were usually seen as opportunities to experiment with self-expression, often sexual in nature. Although not explicitly located in the context of a party, Fantomina's adoption of various disguises – her identity concealed through costuming, make-up and carefully modulated body language – evokes the idea of a liberating, albeit dangerous, masquerade. Likewise, eighteenth-century readers had access to racy poetry and bawdy songs, sexually suggestive plays and amatory novels and various types of erotic and pornographic texts.

Fantomina participates in the genre of amatory fiction, a label that usually refers to texts featuring extensive, specific attention to scenes of courtship and seduction. The amount of detail included about these seductions – including careful descriptions of clothing, the exposed parts of a woman's body and oblique descriptions of sexual acts – varied between authors and texts, but usually stopped just short of being explicit. Readers also enjoyed novels with more explicit detail, such as John Cleland's *Memoirs of a Woman of Pleasure* (1748), and writings ranging from the Facebook of London prostitutes, *Harris's List of Covent Garden Ladies*, to a French erotic story called *Le Sopha*, which Haywood translated into English with her collaborator William Hatchett. Haywood's first novel, *Love in Excess*, published in 1719, also highlights seduction and intercourse in more detail, providing titillating glimpses of fulfilled and thwarted desire for men and women.

Thus, it is notable that Haywood provides very little detail about the initial act of sexual contact between Beauplaisir and Fantomina, writing only 'in fine, she was undone'. Importantly, however, she does provide a glimpse into Fantomina's internal life and sexual desires. After the first evening Fantomina spends alone with Beauplaisir, she is flattered and aroused by his attention. Yet the act of penetration which occurs the subsequent night is implied to be involuntary. Fantomina 'struggled all she could', but her inability or unwillingness to reveal herself as an heiress rather than a whore renders her a victim to Beauplaisir's sexual desires. Instead of dwelling upon her ruin and dissolving into despair after the loss of her virginity outside of marriage, though, Fantomina decides that she quite enjoyed the attention (if not the sex as well). This leads to the remainder of the novella, in which her sexual adventures highlight her creativity, ingenuity and daring pursuit of physical pleasure until her inevitable extramarital pregnancy and banishment.

Many modern readers struggle with interpreting a sexual relationship that begins with rape and ends with an unwanted pregnancy and abandonment as a generative one. These plot points are undeniable, but her projected future as the resident of a French convent is far from the restrictive fate we might first imagine. Enclosed Catholic spaces like monasteries and convents were frequently associated with excessive sexuality and lax behaviour among eighteenth-century English readers, due in no small part to anti-Catholic sentiment and a prevailing discomfort with single-sex institutions. By positing Fantomina as destined for exile in a country that was viewed as more sexually permissive (France) and in a social setting that was stereotypically assumed to have less supervision over women (the convent), Haywood may have intended to offer hope for Fantomina as an independent woman. For its nuanced portrayal of young womanhood, its sympathy for – if not always approval of – female sexuality and its tantalising hints at a world beyond hidebound social mores, *Fantomina* is deservedly ranked among not only Haywood's greatest works, but the most significant pieces of fiction from the eighteenth century.

As we mentioned earlier, *Fantomina*'s significance hasn't always been recognised. Literary scholarship in the nineteenth and twentieth centuries about eighteenth-century writing tends to erase Haywood and other women writers' contributions in favour of a narrative about 'great' male writers creating the novel and other fictional modes. A more accurate understanding of the complex print market in the eighteenth century has since emerged through study of these previously over-looked works. Feminist literary critics, in particular, pushed to recover texts by neglected women authors, and Haywood's work returned to print in the 1980s. Since this period of recovery, interpretations of her work as wildly feminist and liberating (to more conservative in her later years) abound, as generations of critics have had more access to a wider array of her writings, along with scholarship about her life and decades-long career.

One of the thorniest issues in *Fantomina* remains the role of consent. As discussed above, Fantomina's first sexual encounter with Beauplaisir slides from an act of seduction to one of rape. Agency, liberation and the boundaries of sexual contact remain just as pertinent today as during Haywood's lifetime: you can see Fantomina as a rape survivor replaying her trauma through her repeated sexual encounters, a woman who 'asked for it' and got what was coming to her, an innocent who didn't think about the larger consequences of her actions, or as a more complicated character. The novella shows readers a layered view of sexual assault and its consequences long before the #metoo movement rose to prominence, as sexual acts become fraught with interpretation both from the participants themselves and their society.

Though Haywood wrote over sixty novels, along with poems, plays, periodicals, translations and histories, *Fantomina* remains one of her best known works today. Widely anthologised and taught in university classrooms across the world (full disclosure: all three of writers of this introduction have taught this text to undergraduates), this story continues to trouble our ideas of masculinity, femininity, consent, sexual performativity, disguise, desire and more. What is the nature of desire? Of disguise? Why and how is women's sexuality regulated in ways markedly different than men's? Who, exactly, is Fantomina, a character whose real name is never mentioned? What is this story trying to teach its readers? Unlike more straightforward, didactic texts of the period – often with plots where a woman is seduced, ruined and then dies as punishment – Haywood's story leaves us curious about what Fantomina's next move will be. As readers of Haywood's fiction 300 years after it was written, this is the kind of plot that leaves us wanting more.

ABOUT THE AUTHORS

DR SARAH CREEL is the Lead Academic Writing Instructor and Director of the Research Communication Certificate in the Graduate School at the University of Alabama at Birmingham. Sarah has over 13 years of research and teaching experience in higher education and a particular love for Eliza Haywood, and is an officer of the International Eliza Haywood Society. She's published on Haywood in a variety of mediums from the *Modern Language Association* to online journals and academic blogs. Her current work on female boxers of the eighteenth century is forthcoming in *English Studies*. She fervently believes that Haywood should be accessible to all.

BETHANY E. QUALLS is a Ph.D. candidate at the University of California, Davis, where she teaches literature and writing courses. She's spent the past two decades in a variety of writing and editorial roles, including as a general academic and textual editor for *The Broadview Anthology of British Literature*. Bethany's research focuses on eighteenth-century print culture, gossip, prostitute narratives, graphic satire, seriality and fashion. She delights in Eliza Haywood's many strange works, is an officer of the International Eliza Haywood Society, and has an essay forthcoming on Haywood's 1725 *The Tea-Table* in the Routledge collection *A Spy on Haywood*.

DR ANNA (KATIE) SAGAL has been teaching eighteenth-century British literature and writing to undergraduates for the past decade and has quite often convinced her students to read *Fantomina*, much to their delight. She is the Vice President of the International Eliza Haywood Society and her published writing on women's literature has included multiple articles on Eliza Haywood's clever strategies for female opportunity and empowerment. Major research projects also focus on women's scientific writing and art of the eighteenth century. Dr Sagal's book, *Botanical Entanglements: Women, Plants, Literature, and Artwork in the Eighteenth Century* is forthcoming from the University of Virginia Press in Autumn 2021. Unsurprisingly, the very first chapter is about Eliza Haywood.

FANTOMINA

OR,

LOVE IN A MAZE

BEING A

Secret History

OF AN

AMOUR

BETWEEN TWO

Persons of Condition

BY MRS ELIZA HAYWOOD

In Love the Victors from the Vanquish'd fly.
They fly that wound, and they pursue that dye.
WALLER*

A YOUNG LADY OF distinguished Birth, Beauty, Wit and Spirit happened to be in a Box one Night at the Playhouse; where, though there were a great Number of celebrated Toasts, she perceived several Gentlemen extremely pleased themselves with entertaining a Woman who sat in a Corner of the Pit, and, by her Air and Manner of receiving them, might easily be known to be one of those who come there for no other Purpose than to create Acquaintance with as many as seem desirous of it. She could not help testifying her Contempt of Men, who, regardless either of the Play or Circle, threw away their Time in such a Manner to some Ladies that sat by her. But they, either less surprised by being more accustomed to such Sights than she, who had been bred for the most Part in the Country, or not of a Disposition to consider anything very deeply, took but little Notice of it. She still thought of it, however; and the longer she reflected on it, the greater was her Wonder that Men, some of whom she knew were accounted to have Wit, should have Tastes so very depraved. – This excited a Curiosity in her to know in what Manner these Creatures were address'd: – She was young, a Stranger to the World, and consequently to the Dangers of it; and, having nobody in Town at that Time to whom she was oblig'd to be accountable for her Actions, did in everything as her Inclinations or Humours render'd most agreeable to her: Therefore thought it not in the least a Fault to put in practice a little Whim which came immediately into her Head: to dress herself as near as she cou'd in the Fashion of those Women who make sale of their Favours, and set herself in the Way of being accosted as such a one, having at that Time no other Aim than the Gratification of an innocent Curiosity. – She no sooner design'd this Frolic than she put it in Execution; and, muffling her Hoods over her Face, went the next Night into the Gallery Box, and, practising as much as she had observ'd at that Distance the Behaviour of that Woman, was not long before she found her Disguise had answer'd the Ends she wore it for: – A Crowd of Purchasers of all Degrees and Capacities were in a Moment gather'd about her, each endeavouring to outbid the other in offering her a Price for her Embraces. – She listen'd to 'em all, and was not a little diverted in her Mind at the Disappointment she shou'd give to so many, each of which thought himself secure of gaining her. – She was told by 'em all that she was the most lovely Woman in the World; and some cry'd, Gad, she is mighty like my fine Lady Such-a-one, – naming her own Name. She was naturally vain, and receiv'd no small Pleasure in hearing herself prais'd, tho' in the Person of another, and a suppos'd Prostitute; but she dispatch'd as soon as she cou'd all that had hitherto attack'd her when she saw the accomplish'd Beauplaisir was making his Way thro' the Crowd as fast as he was able to reach the Bench she sat on. She had often seen him in the Drawing Room,* had talk'd with him; but then her Quality and reputed Virtue kept him from using her with that Freedom she now expected he wou'd do, and had discover'd some-thing in him which had made her often think she shou'd not be displeas'd if he wou'd abate some Part of his Reserve. – Now was the Time to have her Wishes answer'd: – He look'd in her Face and fancy'd, as many others had done, that she very much resembled that Lady whom she really was; but the vast Disparity there appear'd between their Characters prevented him from entertaining even the most distant Thought that they cou'd be the same. – He address'd her at first with the usual Salutations of her pretended Profession, as – Are you engag'd, Madam? – Will you permit me to wait on you home after the Play? – By Heaven, you are a fine Girl! – How long have you us'd this House? – and such like Questions; but perceiving she had a Turn of Wit and a genteel Manner in her Raillery, beyond what is frequently to be found among those Wretches who are for the most part Gentlewomen but by Necessity, few of 'em having had an Education suitable to what they affect to appear, he chang'd the Form of his Conversation, and show'd her it was not because he understood no better that he had made use of Expressions so little polite. – In fine, they were infinitely charm'd with each other: He was transported to find so much Beauty and Wit in a Woman who he doubted not but on very easy Terms he might enjoy; and she found a vast deal of Pleasure in conversing with him in this free and unrestrain'd Manner. They pass'd their Time all the Play with an equal Satisfaction; but when it was over, she found herself involv'd in a Difficulty which before never enter'd into her Head, but which she knew not well how to get over. – The Passion he profess'd for her was not of that humble Nature which can be content with distant Adorations: – He resolv'd not to part from her without the Gratifications of those Desires she had inspir'd; and, presuming on the Liberties which her suppos'd Function allow'd of, told her she must either go with him to some convenient House of his procuring or permit him to wait on her to her own Lodgings. – Never had she been in such a Dilemma: Three or four Times did she open her Mouth to confess her real Quality; but the Influence of her ill Stars prevented it by putting an Excuse into her Head, which did the Business as well, and at the same Time did not take from her the Power of seeing and entertaining him a second Time with the same Freedom she had done this. – She told him she was under Obligations to a Man who maintain'd her, and whom she durst not disappoint, having promis'd to meet him that Night at a House hard by. – This Story, so like what those Ladies sometimes tell, was not at all suspected by Beauplaisir; and assuring her he wou'd be far from doing her a Prejudice, desir'd that, in return for the Pain he shou'd suffer in being depriv'd of her Company that Night, that she wou'd order her Affairs so as not to render him unhappy the next. She gave a solemn Promise to be in the same Box on the Morrow Evening; and they took Leave of each other; he to the Tavern to drown the Remembrance of his Disappointment; she in a Hackney Chair hurry'd home to indulge Contemplation on the Frolic she had taken, designing nothing less on her first Reflections than to keep the Promise she had made him, and hugging herself with Joy that she had the good Luck to come off undiscover'd.

BUT THESE COGITATIONS were but of a short Continuance; they vanish'd with the Hurry of her Spirits, and were succeeded by others vastly different and ruinous: – All the Charms of Beauplaisir came fresh into her Mind; she languish'd, she almost dy'd for another Opportunity of conversing with him; and not all the Admonitions of her Discretion were effectual to oblige her to deny laying hold of that which offer'd itself the next Night. – She depended on the Strength of her Virtue to bear her safe thro'

Trials more dangerous than she apprehended this to be, and, never having been address'd by him as Lady, – was resolv'd to receive his Devoirs as a Town-Mistress, imagining a world of Satisfaction to herself in engaging him in the Character of such a one, and in observing the Surprise he would be in to find himself refused by a Woman who he supposed granted her Favours without Exception. – Strange and unaccountable were the Whimsies she was possess'd of, – wild and incoherent her Desires, – unfix'd and undetermin'd her Resolutions, but in that of seeing Beauplaisir in the Manner she had lately done. As for her Proceedings with him, or how a second Time to escape him without discovering who she was, she cou'd neither assure herself, nor whither or not in the last Extremity she wou'd do so. – Bent, however, on meeting him, whatever shou'd be the Consequence, she went out some Hours before the Time of going to the Playhouse, and took Lodgings in a House not very far from it, intending that, if he shou'd insist on passing some Part of the Night with her, to carry him there, thinking she might with more Security to her Honour entertain him at a Place where she was Mistress than at any of his own choosing.

THE APPOINTED HOUR being arriv'd, she had the Satisfaction to find his Love in his Assiduity: He was there before her; and nothing cou'd be more tender than the Manner in which he accosted her: But from the first Moment she came in, to that of the Play being done, he continued to assure her no Consideration shou'd prevail with him to part from her again as she had done the Night before; and she rejoic'd to think she had taken that Precaution of providing herself with a Lodging, to which she thought she might invite him without running any Risk either of her Virtue or Reputation. – Having told him she wou'd admit of his accompanying her home, he seem'd perfectly satisfy'd; and leading her to the Place, which was not above twenty Houses distant, wou'd have order'd a Collation to be brought after them. But she wou'd not permit it, telling him she was not one of those who suffer'd themselves to be treated at their own Lodgings; and as soon she was come in sent a Servant belonging to the House to provide a very handsome Supper, and Wine, and everything was serv'd to Table in a Manner which show'd the Director neither wanted Money, nor was ignorant how it shou'd be laid out.

THIS PROCEEDING, though it did not take from him the Opinion that she was what she appeared to be, yet it gave him Thoughts of her, which he had not before. – He believ'd her a *Mistress*, but believ'd her to be one of a superior Rank, and began to imagine the Possession of her would be much more Expensive than at first he had expected: But not being of a Humour to grudge anything for his Pleasures, he gave himself no further Trouble than what were occasioned by Fears of not having Money enough to reach her Price about him.

SUPPER BEING OVER, which was intermixed with a vast deal of amorous Conversation, he began to explain himself more than he had done; and both by his Words and Behaviour let he know he would not be denied that Happiness the Freedoms she allow'd had made him hope. – It was in vain; she would have retracted the Encouragement she had given: – In vain she endeavoured to delay till the next Meeting the fulfilling of his Wishes: – She had now gone too far to retreat: – *He* was bold; – he was resolute: *She* fearful, – confus'd, altogether unprepar'd to resist in such Encounters, and rendered more so by the extreme Liking she had to him.

– Shock'd, however, at the Apprehension of really losing her Honour, she struggled all she could, and was just going to reveal the whole Secret of her Name and Quality when the Thoughts of the Liberty he had taken with her, and those he still continued to prosecute, prevented her, with representing the Danger of being expos'd and the whole Affair made a Theme for public Ridicule. – Thus much, indeed, she told him: that she was a Virgin, and had assumed this Manner of Behaviour only to engage him. But that he little regarded, or if he had, would have been far from obliging him to desist; – nay, in the present burning Eagerness of Desire, 'tis probable that, had he been acquainted both with who and what she really was, the Knowledge of her Birth would not have influenc'd him with Respect sufficient to have curb'd the wild Exuberance of his luxurious Wishes, or made him in that longing, – that impatient Moment, change the Form of his Addresses. In fine, she was undone; and he gain'd a Victory so highly rapturous that, had he known over whom, scarce could he have triumphed more. Her Tears, however, and the Distraction she appeared in after the ruinous Ecstasy was past, as it heighten'd his Wonder, so it abated his Satisfaction: – He could not imagine for what Reason a Woman, who, if she intended not to be a *Mistress*, had counterfeited the Part of one, and taken so much Pains to engage him, should lament a Consequence which she could not but expect, and till the last Test seem'd inclinable to grant; and was both surpris'd and troubled at the Mystery. – He omitted nothing that he thought might make her easy; and, still retaining an Opinion that the Hope of Interest had been the chief Motive which had led her to act in the Manner she had done, and believing that she might know so little of him as to suppose, now she had nothing left to give, he might not make that Recompense she expected for her Favours: To put her out of that Pain, he pulled out of his Pocket a Purse of Gold, entreating her to accept of that as an Earnest of what he intended to do for her; assuring her, with ten thousand Protestations, that he would spare nothing which his whole Estate could purchase to procure her Content and Happiness. This Treatment made her quite forget the Part she had assum'd, and throwing it from her with an Air of Disdain: Is this a Reward (*said she*) for Condescensions such as I have yielded to? – Can all the Wealth you are possess'd of make a Reparation for my Loss of Honour? – Oh! no, I am undone beyond the Power of Heaven itself to help me! – She uttered many more such Exclamations, which the amaz'd Beauplaisir heard without being able to reply to, till, by Degrees sinking from that Rage of Temper, her Eyes resumed their softening Glances, and, guessing at the Consternation he was in: No, my dear Beauplaisir (*added she*), your Love alone can compensate for the Shame you have involved me in; be you sincere and constant, and I hereafter shall, perhaps, be satisfy'd with my Fate, and forgive myself the Folly that betray'd me to you.

BEAUPLAISIR THOUGHT HE could not have a better Opportunity than these Words gave him of enquiring who she was, and wherefore she had feigned herself to be of a Profession which he was now convinc'd she was not; and after he had made her a thousand Vows of an Affection, as inviolable and ardent as she could wish to find in him, entreated she would inform him by what Means his Happiness had been brought about, and also to whom he was indebted for the Bliss he had enjoy'd. – Some Remains of yet unextinguished Modesty and Sense of Shame made her blush exceedingly at this Demand; but recollecting herself in a little Time, she told him so much of the Truth as to what related to the Frolic she had taken of satisfying her Curiosity in what Manner *Mistresses*, of the Sort she appeared to be, were treated by those who addressed them; but forbore discovering her true Name and Quality, for the Reasons she had done before, resolving, if he boasted of this Affair, he should not have it in his Power to touch her Character: she therefore said she was the Daughter of a Country Gentleman who was come to Town to buy Clothes, and that she was call'd Fantomina. He had no Reason to distrust the Truth of this Story, and was therefore satisfy'd with it; but did not doubt by the Beginning of her Conduct but that in the End she would be in Reality the Thing she so artfully had counterfeited; and had good Nature enough to pity the Misfortunes he imagin'd would be her Lot: but to tell her so, or offer his Advice in that Point, was not his Business – at least, as yet.

THEY PARTED NOT till towards Morning; and she oblig'd him to a willing Vow of visiting her the next Day at Three in the Afternoon. It was too late for her to go home that Night, therefore contented herself with lying there. In the Morning she sent for the Woman of the House to come up to her, and, easily perceiving by her Manner that she was a Woman who might be influenced by Gifts, made her a Present of a Couple of Broad Pieces, and desir'd her, that if the Gentleman who had been there the Night before should ask any Questions concerning her, that he should be told she was lately come out of the Country, had lodg'd there about a Fortnight and that her Name was Fantomina. I shall (*also added she*) lie but seldom here; nor, indeed, ever come but in those Times when I expect to meet him: I would, therefore, have you order it so that he may think I am but just gone out if he should happen by any Accident to call when I am not here; for I would not for the World have him imagine I do not constantly lodge here. The Landlady assur'd her she would do everything as she desired, and gave her to understand she wanted not the Gift of Secrecy.

EVERYTHING BEING ORDERED at this Home for the Security of her Reputation, she repaired to the other, where she easily excused to an unsuspecting

Aunt with whom she boarded her having been abroad all Night, saying she went with a Gentleman and his Lady in a Barge to a little Country Seat of theirs up the River, all of them designing to return the same Evening; but that one of the Bargemen happ'ning to be taken ill on the sudden, and no other Waterman to be got that Night, they were oblig'd to tarry till Morning. Thus did this Lady's Wit and Vivacity assist her in all but where it was most needful. – She had Discernment to foresee and avoid all those Ills which might attend the Loss of her Reputation, but was wholly blind to those of the Ruin of her Virtue; and having managed her Affairs so as to secure the one, grew perfectly easy with the Remembrance she had forfeited the other. – The more she reflected on the Merits of Beauplaisir, the more she excused herself for what she had done; and the Prospect of that continued Bliss she expected to share with him took from her all Remorse for having engaged in an Affair which promised her so much Satisfaction, and in which she found not the least Danger of Misfortune. – If he is really (*said she to herself*) the faithful, the constant Lover he has sworn to be, how charming will be our Amour? – And if he should be false, grow satiated, like other Men, I shall but, at the worst, have the private Vexation of knowing I have lost him; – the Intrigue being a Secret, my Disgrace will be so too: – I shall hear no Whispers as I pass – She is Forsaken! – The odious Word Forsaken will never wound my Ears; nor will my Wrongs excite either the Mirth or Pity of the talking World: – It will not be even in the Power of my Undoer himself to triumph over me; and while he laughs at, and perhaps despises the fond, the yielding Fantomina, he will revere and esteem the virtuous, the reserv'd Lady. – In this Manner did she applaud her own Conduct and exult with the Imagination that she had more Prudence than all her Sex beside. And it must be confessed, indeed, that she preserved an Economy in the management of this Intrigue beyond what almost any Woman but herself ever did: In the first Place, by making no Person in the World a Confidant in it; and in the next, in concealing from Beauplaisir himself the Knowledge who she was; for though she met him three or four Days in a Week at that Lodging she had taken for that Purpose, yet as much as he employ'd her Time and Thoughts, she was never miss'd from any Assembly she had been accustomed to frequent. – The Business of her Love has engross'd her till Six in the Evening, and before Seven she has been dress'd in a different Habit, and in another Place. – Slippers and a Nightgown loosely flowing has been the Garb in which he has left the languishing Fantomina; – Lac'd and adorn'd with all the Blaze of Jewels has he, in less than an Hour after, beheld at the Royal Chapel, the Palace Gardens, Drawing Room, Opera or Play the Haughty Awe-inspiring Lady – A thousand Times has he stood amaz'd at the prodigious Likeness between his little Mistress and this Court Beauty; but was still as far from imagining they were the same as he was the first Hour he had accosted her in the Playhouse, though it is not impossible but that her Resemblance to this celebrated Lady might keep his Inclination alive something longer than otherwise they would have been; and that it was to the Thoughts of this (as he supposed) unenjoy'd Charmer she ow'd in great measure the Vigour of his latter Caresses.

BUT HE VARIED not so much from his Sex as to be able to prolong Desire to any great Length after Possession: The rifled Charms of Fantomina soon lost their Poignancy, and grew tasteless and insipid; and when the Season of the Year inviting the Company to the Bath, she offer'd to accompany him, he made an Excuse to go without her. She easily perceiv'd his Coldness, and the Reason why he pretended her going would be inconvenient, and endur'd as much from the Discovery as any of her Sex could do: She dissembled it, however, before him, and took her Leave of him with the Show of no other Concern than his Absence occasion'd: But this she did to take from him all Suspicion of her following him, as she intended, and had already laid a Scheme for. – From her first finding out that he design'd to leave her behind, she plainly saw it was for no other Reason than that, being tir'd of her Conversation, he was willing to be at liberty to pursue new Conquests; and wisely considering that Complaints, Tears, Swoonings and all the Extravagancies which Women make use of in such Cases have little Prevailance over a Heart inclin'd to rove, and only serve to render those who practise them more contemptible, by robbing them of that Beauty which alone can bring back the fugitive Lover, she resolved to take another Course; and remembering the Height of Transport she enjoyed when the agreeable Beauplaisir kneel'd at her Feet, imploring her first Favours, she long'd to prove the same again. Not but a Woman of her Beauty and Accomplishments might have beheld a Thousand in that Condition Beauplaisir had been; but with her Sex's Modesty, she had not also thrown off another Virtue equally valuable, tho' generally unfortunate, *Constancy*: She loved Beauplaisir; it was only he whose Solicitations could give her Pleasure; and, had she seen the whole Species despairing, dying for her sake, it might, perhaps, have been a Satisfaction to her Pride, but none to her more tender Inclination. – Her Design was once more to engage him, to hear him sigh, to see him languish, to feel the strenuous Pressures of his eager Arms, to be compelled, to be sweetly forc'd to what she wished with equal Ardour, was what she wanted, and what she had form'd a Stratagem to obtain, in which she promis'd herself Success.

SHE NO SOONER heard he had left the Town than, making a Pretence to her Aunt that she was going to visit a Relation in the Country, went towards Bath, attended but by two Servants, who she found Reasons to quarrel with on the Road and discharg'd: Clothing herself in a Habit she had brought with her, she forsook the Coach and went into a Wagon, in which Equipage she arriv'd at Bath. The Dress she was in was a round-ear'd Cap, a short Red Petticoat and a little Jacket of Grey Stuff; all the rest of her Accoutrements were answerable to these, and join'd with a broad Country Dialect, a rude unpolish'd Air, which she, having been bred in these Parts, knew very well how to imitate, with her Hair and Eyebrows black'd, made it impossible for her to be known, or taken for any other than what she seem'd. Thus disguis'd did she offer herself to Service in the House where Beauplaisir lodg'd, having made it her Business to find out immediately where he was. Notwithstanding this Metamorphosis she was still extremely pretty; and the Mistress of the House happening at that Time to want a Maid, was very glad of the Opportunity of taking her. She was presently receiv'd into the Family; and had a Post in it (such as she would have chose, had she been left at her Liberty): that of making the Gentlemen's Beds, getting them their Breakfasts and waiting on them in their Chambers. Fortune in this Exploit was extremely on her side; there were no others of the Male Sex in the House than an old Gentleman, who had lost the Use of his Limbs with the Rheumatism, and had come thither for the Benefit of the Waters, and her belov'd Beauplaisir; so that she was in no Apprehensions of any Amorous Violence but where she wish'd to find it. Nor were her Designs disappointed: He was fir'd with the first Sight of her; and tho' he did not presently take any further Notice of her than giving her two or three hearty Kisses, yet she, who now understood that Language but too well, easily saw they were the Prelude to more substantial Joys. – Coming the next Morning to bring his Chocolate, as he had order'd, he catch'd her by the pretty Leg, which the Shortness of her Petticoat did not in the least oppose; then, pulling her gently to him, ask'd her: How long she had been at Service? – How many Sweethearts she had? If she had ever been in Love? and many other such Questions befitting one of the Degree she appear'd to be: All which she answer'd with such seeming Innocence as more en-flam'd the amorous Heart of him who talk'd to her. He compelled her to sit in his Lap; and, gazing on her blushing Beauties, which, if possible, receiv'd Addition from her plain and rural Dress, he soon lost the Power of containing himself. – His wild

Desires burst out in all his Words and Actions; he call'd her little Angel, Cherubim, swore he must enjoy her, though Death were to be the Consequence, devour'd her Lips, her Breasts with greedy Kisses, held to his burning Bosom her half-yielding, half-reluctant Body, nor suffer'd her to get loose till he had ravaged all, and glutted each rapacious Sense with the sweet Beauties of the pretty Celia, for that was the Name she bore in this second Expedition. – Generous as Liberality itself to all who gave him Joy this way, he gave her a handsome Sum of Gold, which she durst not now refuse, for fear of creating some Mistrust, and losing the Heart she so lately had regain'd; therefore taking it with an humble Curtsy, and a well counterfeited Show of Surprise and Joy, cry'd, O Law, Sir! What must I do for all this? He laughed at her Simplicity, and, kissing her again, tho' less fervently than he had done before, bade her not be out of the Way when he came home at Night. She promis'd she would not, and very obediently kept her Word.

HIS STAY AT BATH exceeded not a Month; but in that Time his suppos'd Country Lass had persecuted him so much with her Fondness that, in spite of the Eagerness with which he first enjoy'd her, he was at last grown more weary of her than he had been of Fantomina; which, she perceiving, would not be troublesome, but quitting her Service, remained privately in the Town till she heard he was on his Return; and in that Time provided herself of another Disguise to carry on a third Plot which her inventing Brain had furnished her with, once more to renew his twice-decay'd Ardours. The Dress she had order'd to be made was such as Widows wear in their first Mourning, which, together with the most afflicted and penitential Countenance that ever was seen, was no small Alteration to her who us'd to seem all Gaiety. – To add to this, her Hair, which she was accustom'd to wear very loose both when Fantomina and Celia, was now ty'd back so straight, and her Pinners* coming so very forward, that there was none of it to be seen. In fine, her Habit and her Air were so much chang'd that she was not more difficult to be known in the rude Country Girl than she was now in the sorrowful Widow.

SHE KNEW THAT Beauplaisir came alone in his Chariot to the Bath, and in the Time of her being Servant in the House where he lodg'd heard nothing of anybody that was to accompany him to London, and hop'd he wou'd return in the same Manner he had gone: She therefore hir'd Horses and a Man to attend her to an Inn about ten Miles on this side Bath, where, having discharg'd them, she waited till the Chariot should come by; which, when it did, and she saw that he was alone in it, she call'd to him that drove it to stop a Moment, and going to the Door saluted the Master with these Words:

THE DISTRESS'D AND WRETCHED, Sir (*said she*), never fail to excite Compassion in a generous Mind; and I hope I am not deceiv'd in my Opinion that yours is such: – You have the Appearance of a Gentleman, and cannot, when you hear my Story, refuse that Assistance which is in your Power to give to an unhappy Woman who, without it, may be render'd the most miserable of all created Beings.

IT WOULD NOT be very easy to represent the Surprise so odd an Address created in the Mind of him to whom it was made. – She had not the Appearance of one who wanted Charity; and what other Favour she requir'd he cou'd not conceive:

But, telling her she might command anything in his Power, gave her Encouragement to declare herself in this Manner: You may judge (*resumed she*) by the melancholy Garb I am in that I have lately lost all that ought to be valuable to Womankind; but it is impossible for you to guess the Greatness of my Misfortune unless you had known my Husband, who was Master of every Perfection to endear him to a Wife's Affections. – But, notwithstanding I look on myself as the most unhappy of my Sex in outliving him, I must so far obey the Dictates of my Discretion as to take care of the little Fortune he left behind him, which, being in the Hands of a Brother of his in London, will be all carry'd off to Holland, where he is going to settle; if I reach not the Town before he leaves it, I am undone for ever. – To which End I left Bristol, the Place where we liv'd, hoping to get a Place in the Stage at Bath, but they were all taken up before I came; and, being, by a Hurt I got in a Fall, render'd incapable of travelling any long Journey on Horseback, I have no Way to go to London, and must be inevitably ruin'd in the Loss of all I have on Earth, without you have good Nature enough to admit me to take Part of your Chariot.

HERE THE FEIGNED WIDOW ended her sorrowful Tale, which had been several Times interrupted by a Parenthesis of Sighs and Groans; and Beauplaisir, with a complaisant and tender Air, assur'd her of his Readiness to serve her in Things of much greater Consequence than what she desir'd of him; and told her it would be an Impossibility of denying a Place in his Chariot to a Lady who he could not behold without yielding one in his Heart. She answered the Compliments he made her but with Tears, which seem'd to stream in such abundance from her Eyes that she could not keep her Handkerchief from her Face one Moment. Being come into the Chariot, Beauplaisir said a thousand handsome Things to persuade her from giving way to so violent a Grief, which, he told her, would not only be destructive to her Beauty, but likewise her Health. But all his Endeavours for Consolement appear'd ineffectual, and he began to think he should have but a dull Journey in the Company of one who seem'd so obstinately devoted to the Memory of her dead Husband that there was no getting a Word from her on any other Theme: – But bethinking himself of the celebrated Story of the Ephesian Matron, it came into his Head to make Trial; she who seem'd equally susceptible of Sorrow, might not also be so too of Love; and having began a Discourse on almost every other Topic, and finding her still incapable of answering, resolv'd to put it to the Proof, if this would have no more Effect to rouse her sleeping Spirits: – With a gay Air, therefore, though accompany'd with the greatest Modesty and Respect, he turned the Conversation, as though without Design, on that Joy-giving Passion, and soon discover'd that was indeed the Subject she was best pleas'd to be entertained with; for on his giving her a Hint to begin upon, never any Tongue run more voluble than hers on the prodigious Power it had to influence the Souls of those possess'd of it, to Actions even the most distant from their Intentions, Principles or Humours. – From that she pass'd to a Description of the Happiness of mutual Affection; – the unspeakable Ecstasy of those who meet with equal Ardency; and represented it in Colours so lively, and disclos'd by the Gestures with which her Words were accompany'd and the Accent of her Voice so true a Feeling of what she said that Beauplaisir, without being as stupid, as he was really the contrary, could not avoid perceiving there were Seeds of Fire not yet extinguish'd in this fair Widow's Soul, which wanted but the kindling Breath of tender Sighs to light into a Blaze. – He now thought himself as fortunate as some Moments before he had the Reverse; and doubted not but that before they parted, he should find a Way to dry the Tears of this lovely Mourner to the Satisfaction of them both. He did not, however, offer, as he had done to Fantomina and Celia, to urge his Passion directly to her, but by a thousand little softening Artifices, which he well knew how to use, gave her leave to guess he was enamour'd. When they came to the Inn where they were to lie, he declar'd himself somewhat more freely, and, perceiving she did not resent it past Forgiveness, grew more encroaching still: – He now took the Liberty of kissing away her Tears and catching the Sighs as they issued from her Lips, telling her if Grief was infectious, he was resolv'd to have his Share; protesting he would gladly exchange Passions with her, and be content to bear her Load of *Sorrow*, if she would as willingly ease the Burden of his *Love*. – She said little in answer to the strenuous Pressures with which at last he ventur'd to enfold her, but not thinking it Decent for the Character she had assum'd to yield so suddenly, and unable to deny both his and her own Inclinations, she counterfeited a fainting, and fell motionless upon his Breast. – He had no great Notion that she was in a real Fit, and the Room they supp'd in happening to have a Bed in it, he took her in his Arms and laid her on it, believing that, whatever her Distemper was, that was the most proper Place to convey her to. – He laid himself down by her, and endeavour'd to bring her to herself; and she was too grateful to her kind Physician at her returning Sense to remove from the Posture he had put her in without his Leave.

IT MAY, PERHAPS, seem strange that Beauplaisir should in such near Intimacies continue still deceiv'd: I know there are Men who will swear it is an Impossibility, and that no Disguise could hinder them from knowing a Woman they had once enjoy'd. In answer to these Scruples, I can only say that besides the Alteration which the Change of Dress made in her, she was so admirably skill'd in the Art of feigning that she had the Power of putting on almost what Face she pleas'd, and knew so exactly how to form her

Behaviour to the Character she represented that all the Comedians at both Playhouses are infinitely short of her Performances: She could vary her very Glances, tune her Voice to Accents the most different imaginable from those in which she spoke when she appear'd herself. – These Aids from Nature, join'd to the Wiles of Art, and the Distance between the Places where the imagin'd Fantomina and Celia were, might very well prevent his having any Thought that they were the same, or that the fair Widow was either of them: It never so much as enter'd his Head, and though he did fancy he observed in the Face of the latter Features which were not altogether unknown to him, yet he could not recollect when or where he had known them; – and, being told by her that from her Birth she had never remov'd from Bristol, a Place where he never was, he rejected the Belief of having seen her, and suppos'd his Mind had been deluded by an Idea of some other whom she might have a Resemblance of.

THEY PASS'D THE TIME of their Journey in as much Happiness as the most luxurious Gratification of wild Desires could make them, and, when they came to the End of it, par_ed not without a mutual Promise of seeing each other often. – He told her to what Place she should direct a Letter to him; and she assur'd him she would send to let him know where to come to her as soon as she was fixed in Lodgings.

SHE KEPT HER PROMISE, and, charm'd with the Continuance of his eager Fondness, went not home, but into private Lodgings, whence she wrote to him to visit her the first Opportunity and enquire for the Widow Bloomer. – She had no sooner dispatched this Billet than she repair'd to the House where she had lodg'd as Fantomina, charging the People if Beauplaisir should come there not to let him know she had been out of Town. From thence she wrote to him, in a different Hand, a long Letter of Complaint, that he had been so cruel in not sending one Letter to her all the Time he had been absent, entreated to see him and concluded with subscribing herself his unalterably Affectionate Fantomina. She received in one Day Answers to both these. The first contain'd these Lines:

To the Charming Mrs Bloomer,

It would be impossible, my Angel, for me to express the thousandth Part of that Infinity of Transport the Sight of your dear Letter gave me. – Never was Woman form'd to charm like you; never did any look like you, write like you, bless like you; – nor did ever Man adore as I do. – Since Yesterday we parted, I have seem'd a Body without a Soul; and had you not by this inspiring Billet gave me new Life, I know not what by Tomorrow I should have been. – I will be with you this Evening about Five: – O! 'tis an Age till then; – But the cursed Formalities of Duty oblige me to Dine with my Lord – who never rises from Table till that Hour; – therefore Adieu till then, sweet lovely Mistress of the Soul and all the Faculties of

   Your most faithful,

BEAUPLAISIR

The other was in this Manner:

To the Lovely Fantomina,

If you were half so sensible as you ought of your own Power of charming, you would be assur'd that to be unfaithful or unkind to you would be among the Things that are in their very Natures Impossibilities. – It was my Misfortune, not my Fault, that you were not persecuted every Post with a

Declaration of my unchanging Passion; but I had unluckily forgot the Name of the Woman at whose House you are, and knew not how to form a Direction that it might come safe to your Hands. – And, indeed, the Reflection how you might misconstrue my Silence brought me to Town some Weeks sooner than I intended. – If you knew how I have languish'd to renew those Blessings I am permitted to enjoy in your Society, you would rather pity than condemn

Your ever faithful,

BEAUPLAISIR

P.S. I fear I cannot see you till Tomorrow; some Business has unluckily fallen out that will engross my Hours till then. – Once more, my Dear, Adieu.

TRAITOR! CRY'D SHE as soon as she had read them, 'tis thus our silly, fond, believing Sex are serv'd when they put Faith in Man: So had I been deceiv'd and cheated, had I like the rest believ'd, and sat down mourning in Absence, and vainly waiting recover'd Tendernesses. – How do some Women (*continued she*) make their Life a Hell, burning in fruitless Expectations, and dreaming out their Days in Hopes and Fears, then wake at last to all the Horror of Despair? – But I have outwitted even the most Subtle of the deceiving Kind, and while he thinks to fool me, is himself the only beguiled Person.

SHE MADE HERSELF, most certainly, extremely happy in the Reflection on the Success of her Stratagems; and while the Knowledge of his Inconstancy and Levity of Nature kept her from having that real Tenderness for him she would else have had, she found the Means of gratifying the Inclination she had for his agreeable Person, in as full a Manner as she could wish. She had all the Sweets of Love, but as yet had tasted none of the Gall, and was in a State of Contentment, which might be envy'd by the more Delicate.

WHEN THE EXPECTED Hour arriv'd, she found that her Lover had lost no part of the Fervency with which he had parted from her; but when the next Day she receiv'd him as Fantomina, she perceiv'd a prodigious Difference; which led her again into Reflections on the Unaccountableness of Men's Fancies, who still prefer the last Conquest, only because it is the last. – Here was an evident Proof of it; for there could not be a Difference in

Merit, because they were the same Person; but the Widow Bloomer was a more new Acquaintance than Fantomina, and therefore esteem'd more valuable. This, indeed, must be said of Beauplaisir: that he had a greater Share of good Nature than most of his Sex, who, for the most part, when they are weary of an Intrigue, break it entirely off, without any Regard to the Despair of the abandon'd Nymph. Though he retain'd no more than a bare Pity and Complaisance for Fantomina, yet believing she lov'd him to an Excess, would not entirely forsake her, though the Continuance of his Visits was now become rather a Penance than a Pleasure.

THE WIDOW BLOOMER triumph'd some Time longer over the Heart of this Inconstant, but at length her Sway was at an End, and she sunk in this Character to the same Degree of Tastelesness as she had done before in that of Fantomina and Celia. – She presently perceiv'd it, but bore it as she had always done; it being but what she expected, she had prepar'd herself for it, and had another Project in embryo, which she soon ripen'd into Action. She did not, indeed, complete it altogether so suddenly as she had done the others, by reason there must be Persons employ'd in it; and the Aversion she had to any Confidants in her Affairs, and the Caution with which she had hitherto acted, and which she was still determin'd to continue, made it very difficult for her to find a Way without breaking thro' that Resolution to compass what she wish'd. – She got over the Difficulty at last, however, by proceeding in a Manner, if possible, more extraordinary than all her former Behaviour: – Muffling herself up in her Hood one Day, she went into the Park about the Hour when there are a great many necessitous Gentlemen who think themselves above doing what they call little Things for a Maintenance, walking in the Mall, to take a Chameleon Treat and fill their Stomachs with Air instead of Meat. Two of those, who by their Physiognomy she thought most proper for her Purpose, she beckon'd to come to her; and taking them into a Walk more remote from Company, began to communicate the Business she had with them in these Words: I am sensible, Gentlemen (*said she*), that, through the Blindness of Fortune and Partiality of the World, Merit frequently goes unrewarded, and that those of the best Pretentions meet with the least Encouragement: – I ask your Pardon (*continued she, perceiving they seem'd surpris'd*), if I am mistaken in the Notion that you two may, perhaps, be of the Number of those who have Reason to complain of the Injustice of Fate; but if you are such as I take you for, have a Proposal to make you, which may be of some little Advantage to you. Neither of them made any immediate Answer, but appear'd bury'd in Consideration for some Moments. At length: We should, doubtless, Madam (*said one of them*), willingly come into any Measures to oblige you, provided they are such as may bring us into no Danger, either as to our Persons or Reputations. That which I require of you (*resumed she*) has nothing in it criminal: All that I desire is Secrecy in what you are entrusted, and to disguise yourselves in such a Manner as you cannot be known if hereafter seen by the Person on whom you are to impose. – In fine, the Business is only an innocent Frolic, but, if blaz'd abroad, might be taken for too great a Freedom in me: – Therefore, if you resolve to assist me, here are five Pieces to drink my Health, and assure you that I have not discours'd you on an Affair I design not to proceed in; and when it is accomplish'd fifty more lie ready for your Acceptance. These Words, and, above all, the Money, which was a Sum which, 'tis probable, they had not seen of a long Time, made them immediately assent to all she desir'd and press for the Beginning of their Employment. But Things were not yet ripe for Execution; and she told them that the next Day they should be let into the Secret, charging them to meet her in the same Place at an Hour she appointed. 'Tis hard to say which of these Parties went away best pleas'd: *they*, that Fortune had sent them so unexpected a Windfall; or *she*, that she had found Persons who appeared so well qualified to serve her.

INDEFATIGABLE IN THE PURSUIT of whatsoever her Humour was bent upon, she had no sooner left her new-engag'd Emissaries than she went in search of a House for the completing of her Project. – She pitch'd on one very large, and magnificently furnished, which she hir'd by the Week, giving them the Money beforehand, to prevent any Inquiries. The next Day she repaired to the Park, where she met the punctual Squires of low Degree; and, ordering them to follow her to the House she had taken, told them they must condescend to appear like Servants, and gave each of them a very rich Livery. Then, writing a Letter to Beauplaisir, in a Character vastly different from either of those she had made use of as Fantomina or the fair Widow Bloomer, order'd one of them to deliver it into his own Hands, to bring back an Answer and to be careful that he sifted out nothing of the Truth. – I do not fear (*said she*) that you should discover to him who I am, because that is a Secret of which you yourselves are ignorant; but I would have you be so careful in your Replies that he may not think the Concealment springs from any other Reasons than your great Integrity to your Trust. – Seem, therefore, to know my whole Affairs; and let your refusing to make him Partaker in the Secret appear to be only the Effect of your Zeal for my Interest and Reputation. Promises of entire Fidelity on the one side, and Reward on the other, being past, the Messenger made what haste he could to the House of Beauplaisir; and, being there told where he might find him, perform'd exactly the Injunction that had been given him. But never Astonishment exceeding that which Beauplaisir felt at the reading this Billet, in which he found these Lines:

To the All-conquering Beauplaisir,

I Imagine not that 'tis a new Thing to you to be told you are the greatest Charm in Nature to our Sex: I shall therefore not to fill up my Letter with any impertinent Praises on your Wit or Person, only tell you that I am infinite in Love with both, and, if you have a Heart not too deeply engag'd, should think myself the happiest of my Sex in being capable of inspiring it with some Tenderness. − There is but one Thing in my Power to refuse you, which is the Knowledge of my Name, which, believing the Sight of my Face will render no Secret, you must not take it ill that I conceal from you. − The Bearer of this is a Person I can trust; send by him your Answer; but endeavour not to dive into the Meaning of this Mystery, which will be impossible for you to unravel, and at the same Time very much disoblige me: − But that you may be in no Apprehensions of being impos'd on by a Woman unworthy of your Regard, I will venture to assure you the first and greatest Men in the Kingdom would think themselves blest to have that Influence over me you have, though unknown to yourself acquir'd. − But I need not go about to raise your Curiosity by giving you any Idea of what my Person is; if you

think fit to be satisfied, resolve to visit me Tomorrow about Three in the Afternoon; and though my Face is hid, you shall not want sufficient Demonstration that she who takes these unusual Measures to commence a Friendship with you is neither Old nor Deform'd. Till then I am,
  Yours,

INCOGNITA

HE HAD SCARCE come to the Conclusion before he ask'd the Person who brought it from what Place he came, the Name of the Lady he serv'd, if she were a Wife, or Widow, and several other Questions directly opposite to the Directions of the Letter; but Silence would have avail'd him as much as did all those Testimonies of Curiosity: No Italian Bravo, employ'd in a Business of the like Nature, perform'd his Office with more Artifice; and the impatient Enquirer was convinc'd that nothing but doing as he was desir'd could give him any Light into the Character of the Woman who declar'd so violent a Passion for him; and, little fearing any Consequence which could ensue from such an Encounter, resolv'd to rest satisfy'd till he was inform'd of everything from herself, not imagining this Incognita varied so much from the

Generality of her Sex as to be able to refuse the Knowledge of anything to the Man she lov'd with that Transcendency of Passion she profess'd, and which his many Successes with the Ladies gave him Encouragement enough to believe. He therefore took Pen and Paper, and answer'd her Letter in Terms tender enough for a Man who had never seen the Person to whom he wrote. The Words were as follows:

To the Obliging and Witty Incognita,
Though to tell me I am happy enough to be lik'd by a Woman such, as by your Manner of Writing, I imagine you to be is an Honour which I can never sufficiently acknowledge, yet I know not how I am able to content myself with admiring the Wonders of your Wit alone: I am certain a Soul like yours must shine in your Eyes with a Vivacity which must bless all they look on. − I shall, however, endeavour to restrain myself in those Bounds you are pleas'd to set me, till by the Knowledge of my inviolable Fidelity I may be thought worthy of gazing on that Heaven I am now but to enjoy in Contemplation. − You need not doubt my glad Compliance with your obliging summons: There is a Charm in your Lines, which gives too sweet an Idea of their lovely Author to be resisted. − I am all impatient for the blissful

*Moment which is to throw me at your Feet, and give me an
Opportunity of convincing you that I am,*
    Your everlasting Slave,

BEAUPLAISIR

NOTHING COULD BE more pleas'd than she, to
whom it was directed, at the Receipt of this Letter;
but when she was told how inquisitive he had been
concerning her Character and Circumstances,
she could not forbear laughing heartily to think
of the Tricks she had play'd him, and applaud-
ing her own Strength of Genius and Force of
Resolution which by such unthought-of Ways
could triumph over her Lover's Inconstancy and
render that very Temper, which to other Women
is the greatest Curse, a Means to make herself
more bless'd. – Had he been faithful to me (*said
she, to herself*), either as Fantomina, or Celia or the
Widow Bloomer, the most violent Passion, if it
does not change its Object, in Time will wither:
Possession naturally abates the Vigour of Desire,
and I should have had, at best, but a cold, insipid,
husband-like Lover in my Arms; but by these Arts
of passing on him as a new Mistress whenever
the Ardour, which alone makes Love a Blessing,

begins to diminish, for the former one, I have him always raving, wild, impatient, longing, dying. – O that all neglected Wives and fond abandon'd Nymphs would take this Method! – Men would be caught in their own Snare and have no Cause to scorn our easy, weeping, wailing Sex! Thus did she pride herself, as if secure she never should have any Reason to repent the present Gaiety of her Humour. The Hour drawing near in which he was to come, she dress'd herself in as magnificent a Manner as if she were to be that Night at a Ball at Court, endeavouring to repair the want of those Beauties which the Vizard should conceal by setting forth the others with the greatest Care and Exactness. Her fine Shape and Air and Neck appear'd to great Advantage; and by that which was to be seen of her, one might believe the rest to be perfectly agreeable. Beauplaisir was prodigiously charm'd, as well with her Appearance as with the Manner she entertain'd him: But though he was wild with Impatience for the Sight of a Face which belong'd to so exquisite a Body, yet he would not immediately press for it, believing before he left her he should easily obtain that Satisfaction. – A noble Collation being over, he began to sue for the Performance of her Promise of granting everything he could ask, excepting the Sight of her Face and Knowledge of her Name. It would have been a ridiculous Piece of Affection in her to have seem'd coy in complying with what she herself had been the first in desiring: She yielded without even a Show of Reluctance: And if there be any true Felicity in an Amour such as theirs, both here enjoy'd it to the full. But not in the Height of all their mutual Raptures could he prevail on her to satisfy his Curiosity with the Sight of her Face: She told him that she hop'd he knew so much of her as might serve to convince him she was not unworthy of his tenderest Regard; and if he cou'd not content himself with that which she was willing to reveal, and which was the Conditions of their meeting, dear as he was to her, she would rather part with him for ever than consent to gratify an Inquisitiveness which, in her Opinion, had no Business with his Love. It was in vain that he endeavour'd to make her sensible of her Mistake, and that this Restraint was the greatest Enemy imaginable to the Happiness of them both: She was not to be persuaded, and he was oblig'd to desist his Solicitations, though determin'd in his Mind to compass what he so ardently desir'd before he left the House. He then turned the Discourse wholly on the Violence of the Passion he had for her; and express'd the greatest Discontent in the World at the Apprehensions of being separated; – swore he could dwell for ever in her Arms, and with such an undeniable Earnestness pressed to be permitted to tarry with her the whole Night, that, had she been less charm'd with his renew'd Eagerness of Desire, she scarce would have had the Power of refusing him; but in granting this Request, she was not without a Thought that he had another Reason for making it besides the Extremity of his Passion, and had it immediately in her Head how to disappoint him.

THE HOURS OF REPOSE being arriv'd, he begg'd she would retire to her Chamber; to which she consented, but oblig'd him to go to Bed first; which he did not much oppose, because he suppos'd she would not lie in her Mask, and doubted not but the Morning's Dawn would bring the wish'd Discovery. – The two imagin'd Servants usher'd him to his new Lodging, where he lay some Moments in all the Perplexity imaginable at the Oddness of this

Adventure. But she suffer'd not these Cogitations to be of any long Continuance: She came, but came in the Dark; which being no more than he expected by the former Part of her Proceedings, he said nothing of; but as much Satisfaction as he found in her Embraces, nothing ever long'd for the Approach of Day with more Impatience than he did. At last it came; but how great was his Disappointment when, by the Noises he heard in the Street, the Hurry of the Coaches and the Cries of Penny-Merchants, he was convinc'd it was Night nowhere but with him. He was still in the same Darkness as before; for she had taken care to blind the Windows in such a manner that not the least Chink was left to let in Day. – He complain'd of her Behaviour in Terms that she would not have been able to resist yielding to if she had not been certain it would have been the Ruin of her Passion: – She, therefore, answered him only as she had done before; and, getting out of the Bed from him, flew out of the Room with too much Swiftness for him to have overtaken her if he had attempted it. The Moment she left him, the two Attendants enter'd the Chamber, and, plucking down the Implements which had screen'd him from the Knowledge of that which he so much desir'd to find out, restored his Eyes once more to Day: – They attended to assist him in Dressing, brought him Tea and by their Obsequiousness let him see there was but one Thing which the Mistress of them would not gladly oblige him in. – He was so much out of Humour, however, at the Disappointment of his Curiosity, that he resolv'd never to make a second Visit. – Finding her in an outer Room, he made no Scruple of expressing the Sense he had of the little Trust she reposed in him, and at last plainly told her he could not submit to receive Obligations from a Lady who thought him incapable of keeping a Secret which she made no Difficulty of letting her Servants into. – He resented, – he once more entreated, – he said all that Man could do to prevail on her to unfold the Mystery; but all his Adjurations were fruitless; and he went out of the House determin'd never to re-enter it till she should pay the Price of his Company with the Discovery of her Face and Circumstances. – She suffer'd him to go with this Resolution, and doubted not but he would recede from it when he reflected on the happy Moments they had pass'd together; but if he did not, she comforted herself with the Design of forming some other Stratagem with which to impose on him a fourth Time.

SHE KEPT THE HOUSE and her Gentlemen Equipage for about a Fortnight, in which Time she continu'd to write to him as Fantomina and the Widow Bloomer, and received the Visits he sometimes made to each; but his Behaviour to both was grown so cold that she began to grow as weary of receiving his now insipid Caresses as he was of offering them: She was beginning to think in what Manner she should drop these two Characters when the sudden Arrival of her Mother, who had been some Time in a foreign Country, oblig'd her to put an immediate Stop to the Course of her whimsical Adventures. – That Lady, who was severely virtuous, did not approve of many Things she had been told of the Conduct of her Daughter; and though it was not in the Power of any Person in the World to inform her of the Truth of what she had been guilty of, yet she heard enough to make her keep her afterwards in a Restraint, little agreeable to her Humour and the Liberties to which she had been accustomed.

BUT THIS CONFINEMENT was not the greatest Part of the Trouble of this now afflicted Lady: She found the Consequences of her amorous Follies would be, without almost a Miracle, impossible to be concealed: – She was with Child; and though she would easily have found Means to have screen'd even this from the Knowledge of the World, had she been at liberty to have acted with the same unquestionable Authority over herself as she did before the coming of her Mother, yet now all her Invention was at a Loss for a Stratagem to impose on a Woman of her Penetration: – By eating little, lacing prodigious straight and the Advantage of a great Hoop Petticoat, however, her Bigness was not taken notice of, and, perhaps, she would not have been suspected till the Time of her going into the Country, where her Mother design'd to send her, and from whence she intended to make her escape to some Place where she might be deliver'd with Secrecy, if the Time of it had not happen'd much sooner than she expected. – A Ball being at Court, the good old Lady was willing she should partake of the Diversion of it as a Farewell to the Town. – It was there she was seiz'd with those Pangs which none in her Condition are exempt from: – She could not conceal the sudden Rack which all at once invaded her; or had her Tongue been mute, her wildly rolling Eyes, the Distortion of her Features and the Convulsions which shook her whole Frame, in spite of her, would have reveal'd she labour'd under some terrible Shock of Nature. – Everybody was surpris'd; everybody was concern'd; but few guessed at the Occasion. – Her Mother, griev'd beyond Expression, doubted not but she was struck with the Hand of Death; and order'd her to be carried Home in a Chair, while herself follow'd in another. – A Physician was immediately sent for: But he, presently perceiving what was her Distemper, call'd the old Lady aside, and told her it was not a Doctor of his Sex, but one of her own her Daughter stood in need of. – Never was Astonishment and Horror greater than that which seiz'd the Soul of this afflicted Parent at these Words: She could not for a Time believe the Truth of what she heard; but he insisting on it, and conjuring her to send for a Midwife, she was at length convinc'd of it. – All the Pity and Tenderness she had been for some Moment before possess'd of now vanish'd, and were succeeded by an adequate Shame and Indignation: – She flew to the Bed where her Daughter was lying, and telling her what she had been inform'd of, and which she was now far from doubting, commanded her to reveal the Name of the Person whose Insinuations had drawn her to this Dishonour. – It was a great while before she could be brought to confess anything, and much longer before she could be prevailed on to name the Man whom she so fatally had lov'd; but the Rack of Nature growing more fierce, and the enraged old Lady protesting no Help should be afforded her while she persisted in her Obstinacy, she, with great Difficulty and Hesitation in her Speech, at last pronounc'd the Name of Beauplaisir. She had no sooner satisfy'd her weeping Mother than that sorrowful Lady sent Messengers at the same Time for a Midwife and for that Gentleman who had occasion'd the other's being wanted. – He happen'd by Accident to be at home, and immediately obey'd the Summons, though prodigiously surpris'd what Business a Lady so much a Stranger to him could have to impart. – But how much greater was his Amazement when, taking him into her Closet, she there acquainted him with her Daughter's Misfortune, of the Discovery she had made and how far he was concern'd in it? – All the Idea one can form of wild Astonishment was mean to what he felt: – He assur'd her that the young Lady her Daughter was a Person whom he had never, more than at a Distance, admir'd: – That he had indeed spoke to her in public Company, but that he never had a Thought which tended to her Dishonour. – His Denials, if possible, added to the Indignation she was before enflam'd with: – She had no longer Patience; and, carrying him into the Chamber, where she was just deliver'd of a fine Girl, cry'd out, I will not be impos'd on: The Truth by one of you shall be reveal'd. – Beauplaisir, being brought to the Bedside, was beginning to address himself to the Lady in it, to beg she would clear the Mistake her Mother was involv'd in; when she, covering herself with the Clothes, and ready to die a second Time with the inward Agitations of her Soul, shriek'd out, O, I am undone! – I cannot live and bear this Shame! – But the old Lady, believing that now or never was the Time to dive into the Bottom of this Mystery, forcing her to rear her Head, told her she should not hope to Escape the Scrutiny of a Parent she had dishonour'd in such a Manner, and, pointing to Beauplaisir: Is this the Gentleman (*said she*) to whom you owe your Ruin? Or have you deceiv'd me by a fictitious Tale? Oh no! (*resum'd the trembling Creature.*) He is, indeed, the innocent Cause of my Undoing: – Promise me your Pardon (*continued she*), and I will relate the Means. Here she ceas'd, expecting what she would reply; which, on hearing Beauplaisir cry out, What mean you, Madam? I your Undoing, who never harbour'd the least Design on you in my Life? she did in these Words: Though the Injury you have done your Family (*said she*) is of a Nature which cannot justly hope Forgiveness, yet be assur'd, I shall much sooner excuse you when satisfied of the Truth than while I am kept in a Suspense, if possible, as vexatious as the Crime itself is to me. Encouraged by this, she related the whole Truth. And 'tis difficult to determine if Beauplaisir or the Lady were most surpris'd at what they heard; he, that he should have been blinded so often by her Artifices; or she, that so young a Creature should have the Skill to make use of them. Both sat for some Time in a profound Reverie; till at length she broke it first in these Words: Pardon, Sir (*said she*), the Trouble I have given you: I must confess it was with a Design to oblige you to repair the supposed Injury you had done this unfortunate Girl by marrying her, but now I know not what to say: – The Blame is wholly hers, and I have nothing to request further of you than that you will not divulge the distracted Folly she has been guilty of. – He answered her in Terms perfectly polite; but made no Offer of that which, perhaps, she expected, though could not, now inform'd of her Daughter's Proceedings, demand. He assured her, however, that if she would commit the new-born Lady to his Care, he would discharge it faithfully. But neither of them would consent to that; and he took his Leave, full of Cogitations, more confus'd than ever he had known in his whole Life. He continued to visit there, to enquire after her Health every Day; but the old Lady, perceiving there was nothing likely to ensue from these Civilities but, perhaps, a Renewing of the Crime, she entreated him to refrain; and as soon as her Daughter was in a Condition, sent her to a Monastery in France, the Abbess of which had been her particular Friend. And thus ended an Intrigue which, considering the Time it lasted, was as full of Variety as any, perhaps, that many Ages has produced.

FINIS

NOTE ON THE TEXT

Fantomina, or, Love in a Maze was first published in 1725 in a collection of Haywood's works, *Secret Histories, Novels and Poems*. The text of this edition is based on the original edition, but in some instances spelling, punctuation and grammar have been silently corrected to make the text more appealing to the modern reader. For the same reason, the eighteenth-century convention of italicising names of people and places has been dropped, given that they are read differently by the contemporary reader, but Haywood's idiosyncratic use of dashes has been retained, along with the original capitalisation, in order to replicate the reading experience of the original text.

NOTES

21   *Waller*: From 'To a Friend' by the English poet and politician Edmund Waller (1606–1687).

25   *Drawing Room*: A formal reception given by a monarch at which ladies were presented at Court.

45   *Pinners*: A close-fitting cap with long flaps on either side, worn by women of higher social status.

www.ingramcontent.com/pod-product-compliance
Lightning Source LLC
Chambersburg PA
CBHW021743190726
48288CB00009B/3143